ADAPTED BY JOHN GREEN

**BASED ON THE SERIES CREATED BY
DAN POVENMIRE & JEFF "SWAMPY" MARSH**

NEW YORK

LIBRARY OF CONGRESS CATALOG CARD NUMBER ON FILE.
978-1-4231-3738-2
FIRST EDITION
10 9 8 7 6 5 4 3 2 1
PRINTED IN THE UNITED STATES OF AMERICA
G658-7729-4-10349

FOR MORE DISNEY PRESS FUN, VISIT WWW.DISNEYBOOKS.COM
VISIT DISNEYCHANNEL.COM

"IT'S ABOUT TIME!"

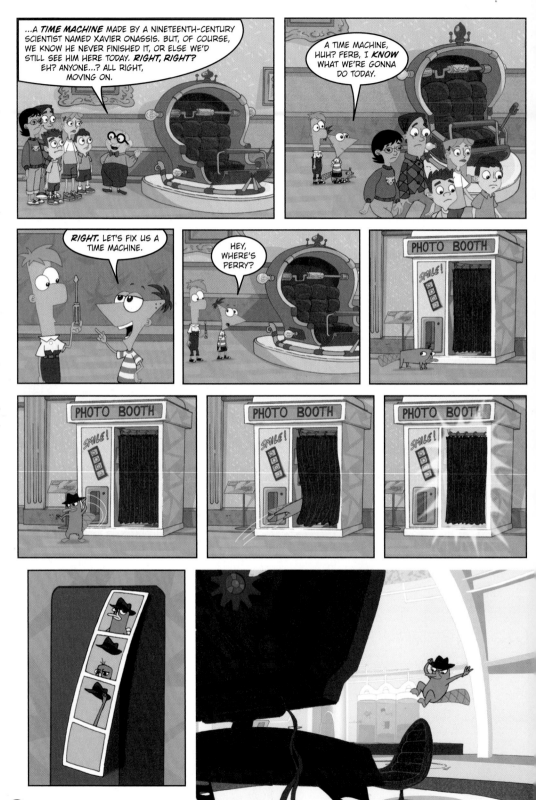

UH, AGENT P? HEY, IT'S ME, CARL, THE INTERN.

WE GOT A BIT OF A SITUATION HERE. MAJOR MONOGRAM HAS BEEN FROZEN LIKE THIS PRETTY MUCH ALL DAY.

SOLID AS A *ROCK.*

ANYHOO, IF THE MAJOR WERE ABLE TO, I'M SURE HE'D SAY DOOFENSHMIRTZ WAS UP TO SOMETHING, AND YOU SHOULD GET TO THE BOTTOM OF IT.

AM I RIGHT? SIR?

MMMMPH...

I'M GONNA TAKE THAT AS A YES! *GOOD LUCK,* AGENT P.

MEANWHILE...

AND *THIS* FOSSIL IS THE *ONLY* REPRESENTATION OF THE GLYKIOLIS SPECIES FROM THE JURASSIC ERA. HOW EXCITING!

GRR...

WHY DO *I* HAVE TO ENDURE THIS *SUFFERING* WHILE PHINEAS AND FERB ARE OFF WHO KNOWS WHERE DOING WHO KNOWS--

--=GASP!=--

5

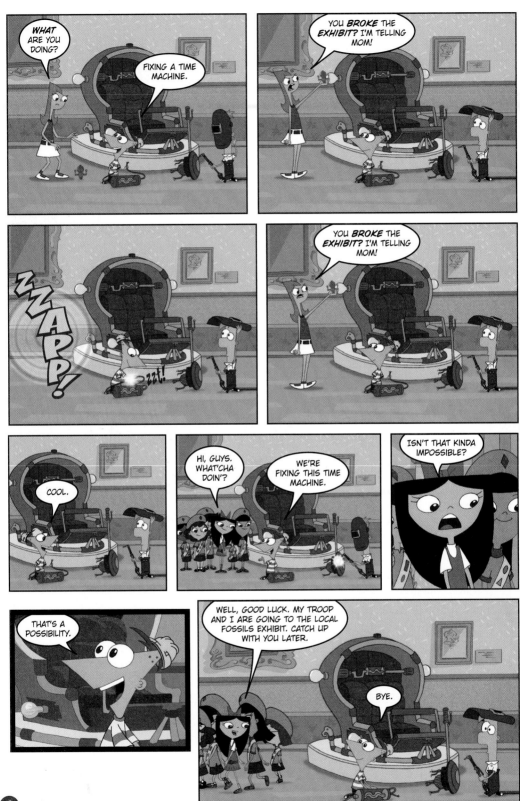

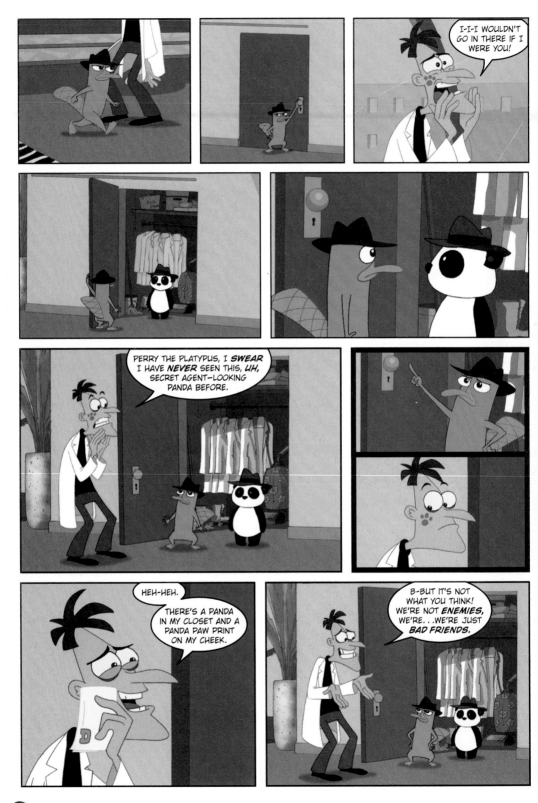

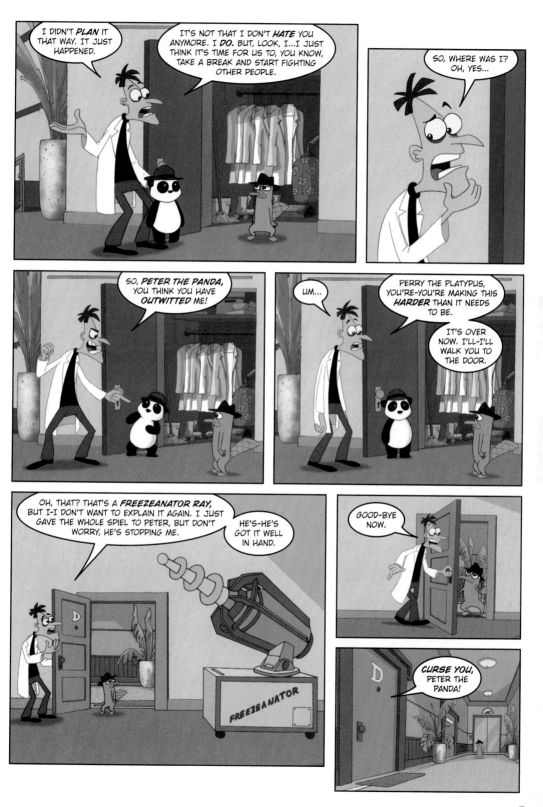

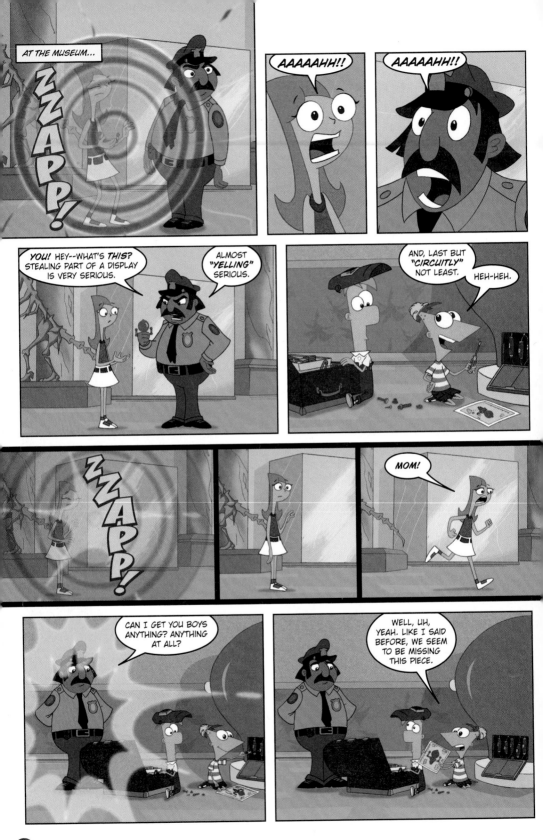

MEANWHILE...

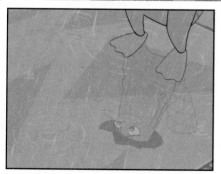

BETTER PANDA RESTAURANT

ACROSS TOWN...

MUSEUM OF NATURAL HISTORY

MOM!

16

22

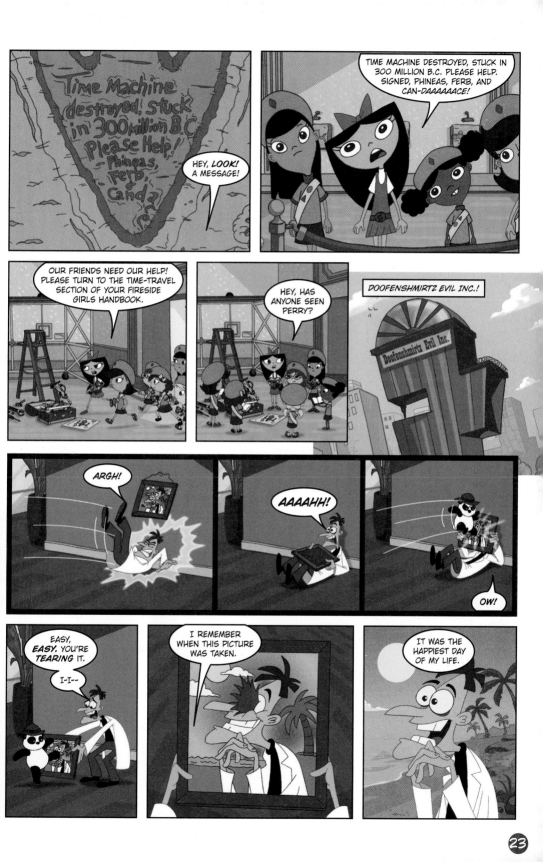